While the Giant is Sleeping...

Alyaa Holston

Suzi Shanahan

CrossRiverkids

Inspired by Cameron, Lauren and Madelyn, who have taught me to look beyond what I am seeing and notice the details. – A.H. –

To Paige and Matthew, as a reminder to always appreciate the beauty surrounding you. – S.S. –

First printing May 2011

ISBN-13: 978-1936501052
ISBN-10: 1936501058

Text copyright 2011 by Alycia Holston. Illustrations copyright 2011 by Suzi Stranahan.
Published by CrossRiver Publishing, Troy, KS 66087

Printed in the U.S.A.

Illustrator's notes: Original artwork was rendered in chalk pastels on artist paper.

While the Giant is Sleeping …

By Alycia Holston

Illustrated by Suzi Stranahan

While the giant is sleeping
the golden sun warms him by day.

The big Montana sky stretches
to the heavens above him.

While the giant is sleeping…

…dark, angry clouds roll over him on waves of thunder. Rain and winds cool the valley, creating a rainbow that fills the sky.

While the giant is sleeping…

…cars travel back and forth along the highway. Some are on their way to visit friends and family, others simply want to gaze upon the mountain as he slumbers.

While the giant is sleeping…

…antelope and elk run up his belly,
hiding between the rocks and trees.
The bighorn sheep keep a watchful
eye on their fun.

While the
	giant is sleeping…

…green trees surround his arms and legs. The tops reach for the sky, protecting the little creatures on the forest floor.

While the giant is sleeping
birds soar and dive over him.

The eagle works hard on her nest
as the geese leave their nests
behind, flying to their
southern homes.

While the giant is sleeping…

…the town below buzzes with excitement.
Sounds of voices and laughter rise to
his ears as children fill the school
yards for a new year.

While the giant is sleeping…

…new fallen snow blankets him in a warm cover.
Tucked in, he feels snug for his long winter nap.

While the giant is sleeping
  the mountains around him glitter
    and glow with their fresh coat of white.

Lake Helena's icy surface creates a perfect reflection of the snowy tops.

While the giant is sleeping…

…the Missouri River rolls past his head, easing its way through the land. The river's long journey to the ocean is just beginning.

While the giant is sleeping…

…wild flowers poke their faces
out of the thawing ground.
Bright, happy colors dress up
the land for spring.

While the giant is sleeping…

…the cows and sheep gather
in the fields by his side.
New babies leap and play
around their grazing mamas.

While the giant is sleeping…

…soft, fluffy clouds tickle
his nose. They sneak up to him
on warm, gentle blowing breezes.

While the giant is sleeping…

…the silvery moon
  shines in his eyes.
Millions of stars decorate
  the enormous night sky.

Facts to Treasure

The Sleeping Giant is located about 10 miles north of Helena, Montana. Montana is known as the Treasure State. Helena is Montana's state capital and many people live there. *Did you see some of the cars people drive when they go by the Giant? How many cars can you count?*

The nose of the Sleeping Giant is called Beartooth Mountain. *Do you think the Giant's nose is bigger than your nose? Can you name some other body parts mentioned in the book?*

The Sleeping Giant is located next to the Gates of the Mountains. Lewis and Clark were explorers that came through the Gates in their boats on the Missouri River. *Did you see the river? What season do you think it is in the picture?*

When people began living in the area, they built houses and barns for their animals. The barns have been there for a long time to protect the animals from the cold and keep their food safe. *What animals were in the picture with the barn? What other kinds of animals live in other places around the Giant?*

Many other mountains surround the Giant while he sleeps. They are called the Big Belt Mountains, Elkhorn Mountains and the Rocky Mountains. *Can you name some of the colors on the mountains?*

Made in the USA
Charleston, SC
25 May 2011